THIS BLOOMSBURY BOOK

BELONGS TO

....

For all the birds in the garden - M

For Stuart and Richard - D

First published in Great Britain in 2004 by Bloomsbury Publishing Plc
38 Soho Square, London, W1D 3HB
This paperback edition first published in 2005

ISBN 0 7475 7132 5

Printed in Hong Kong/China

1 3 5 7 9 10 8 6 4 2

All papers used by Bloomsbury Publishing are natural, recyclable products
made from wood grown in well-managed forests. The manufacturing processes
conform to the environmental regulations of the country of origin.

Yellow Bird, Black Spider

Dosh and Mike Archer

BLOOMSBURY
CHILDREN'S
BOOKS

Yellow Bird,
blue boat

'I like to sail, actually,'
said Yellow Bird.

Yellow Bird,
white hotel

'Why don't you
make a lovely, cosy nest?'
asked Black Spider.

'I like hotels, actually,' said Yellow Bird.

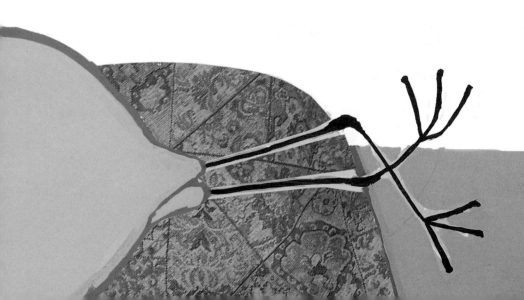

Yellow Bird, red guitar

'Why don't you
sing *tweet, tweet, tweet,*
in a beautiful way?'
asked Black Spider.

'I like to strum, actually,'
said Yellow Bird.

'I like dancing on the beach,
the feel of sand on my toes . . .

I like peace and quiet, vanilla ice-cream,

having baths, and wearing
stripy socks.'

'Birds don't usually
wear stripy socks,'
said Black Spider.

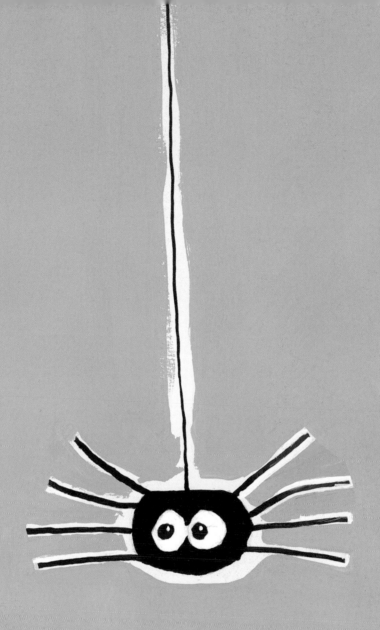

Yellow Bird,
Black Spider

'Why don't you eat
some yummy, squelchy worms?'
asked Black Spider.

'Actually,' said Yellow Bird,

'*I like to eat spiders.*'

Enjoy more great picture books from Bloomsbury Children's Books ...

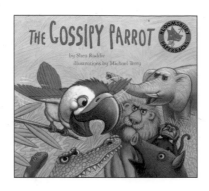

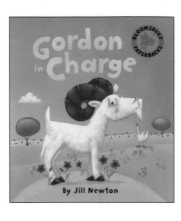

THE GOSSIPY PARROT
Shen Roddie and Michael Terry

GORDON IN CHARGE
Jill Newton

GET BUSY THIS SUMMER!
Stephen Waterhouse

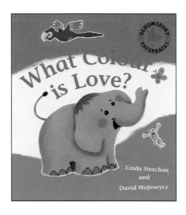

MARVIN WANTED MORE!
Joseph Theobald

WHAT COLOUR IS LOVE?
Linda Strachan and David Wojtowycz

All now available in paperback